WITHDRAWN

P9-DLZ-787

DINO-MIKE

AND THE
MUSEUM MAYHEM

WRITTEN & ILLUSTRATED BY FRANCO

STONE ARCH BOOKS
a capstone imprint

Dino-Mike! is published by
Stone Arch Books,
a Capstone imprint
1710 Roe Crest Drive
North Mankato, Minnesota 56003
www.capstoneyoungreaders.com

Copyright © 2015 by Stone Arch Books

All rights reserved. No part of this publication may
be reproduced in whole or in part, or stored in a
retrieval system, or transmitted in any form or
by any means, electronic, mechanical, photocopying,
recording, or otherwise, without written permission
of the publisher.

Cataloging-in-Publication Data is available on the
Library of Congress website.

ISBN: 978-1-4342-9628-3 (library binding)
ISBN: 978-1-4342-9632-0 (paperback)
ISBN: 978-1-4965-0166-0 (eBook)

Summary: Dino-Mike is at the Museum of Natural
History in this chapter book adventure! Soon, baby
dinos are running wild all over the museum!

Printed in Canada.
092014   008478FRS15

CONTENTS

DINO-MIKE

Young Michael Evans travels the world with his dino-huntin' dad. From the Jurassic Coast in Great Britain to the Liaoning Province in China, young Dino-Mike has been there, *dug* that!

When his dad is dusting fossils, Mike's boning up on his own dino skills — only he's finding the real deal. A live T. rex egg! A portal to the Jurassic period!! An undersea dinosaur sanctuary!!!

Prepare yourself for another wild and wacky Dino-Mike adventure, which nobody will ever believe . . .

Chapter 1
ON GUARD

"Where do you think you're going?"

Mike looked up to see someone staring at him. He was scowling, his face scrunchy and squeezed like a sponge.

Except he wasn't a sponge. He was a big man with a big mustache. It looked extra hairy, as if someone had placed a push broom on his upper lip.

"The museum is closed! You can't go in," the security guard insisted.

"No, no!" a voice from down the hall shouted. Mike stood on his tippy-toes and craned his neck, so he could see over the arm of the guard. "It's okay," continued the voice. "They're with me."

7

Wearing a white laboratory coat,
Dr. Giovanni came running down the
museum corridor, waving his hand.
"They're my guests!" he repeated.

"Sorry, Dr. Giovanni," said the guard.
"They're not on the list. They cannot
enter the museum during off hours."

"Nonsense," said Dr. Giovanni. He placed his hands on Mike's shoulder in an almost protective manner. "Don't you know who this is?"

The look on the security guard's face told everybody that he did not.

"This young man has made the most important dinosaur discovery in the last fifty years!" Mike was convinced at this point that Dr. Giovanni was talking about somebody else. "This young man discovered the T. rex eggs that will be displayed this weekend!"

"Really?" The guard squinted, inspecting Mike from head to toe.

"Certainly," Dr. Giovanni said. "And this is his father, the renowned paleontologist Dr. Stanley Evans."

Mike's father stepped forward and shook hands with the guard. "Hello there," he said. "Very nice to meet you."

"Obviously, Dr. Evans, you've been here before," said Dr. Giovanni, "but I believe this is your son's first visit."

"Yep, that's right," answered Mike.

"Well then," began Dr. Giovanni as he moved down the hall and opened a large door. "Let me be the first to welcome you to New York City and the Museum of Natural History!"

Mike and his dad stepped inside.

"Thank you so much for inviting us," Mike said.

"Nonsense! It's the least we can do for our newest and youngest paleontologist," replied Dr. Giovanni.

"Me? A paleontologist?" Mike asked.

"Of course. You are credited with finding the eggs," Dr. Giovanni replied, gesturing to a glass display case.

There they were — the four eggs Mike had found on his first dino dig. The eggs were roughly the size of softballs. He had discovered them on his last Dino-Mike adventure!

That day, Mike also discovered a real-life T. rex, a mysterious and possibly time-traveling girl named Shannon, and an evil kid named Jurassic Jeff. Jeff had wanted to release real dinosaurs back into modern-day society.

"So yes, when you make a discovery such as this," said Dr. Giovanni, interrupting Mike's thoughts, "we tend to call you an honorary paleontologist."

While Dr. Giovanni had been talking, the security guard and his mustache moved next to Mike. He leaned in to take a closer look at the eggs. "Where did you say you found these?" he asked.

"On my first dino dig," answered Mike, startled by the guard.

The guard stood up straight and rubbed his chin. "And this was just a few weeks ago?" he asked, curious.

TYRANOSAURUS EGGS

"Yes," said Mike's father. "The other paleontologists, including myself, missed them. I'm lucky Mike was there!"

"Interesting," said the guard, twisting one end of his mustache.

"Indeed," agreed Dr. Giovanni. "Now let's head to the laboratory to learn a little more about them. Mike, if you would like to stay on this level to look around for a bit —"

"No, sir!" interrupted Mr. Broom Mustache Security Guard in a stern voice. "The museum is not officially open. We cannot have anybody in this section right now."

"Of course," Dr. Giovanni apologized. "I'm sorry, Mike, but rules are rules, and Mr. Broome does have a job to do."

Mike tried not to laugh. He found it funny that the person he just nicknamed "Broom Mustache Security Guard" was actually named Mr. Broome.

"No problem, Doctor," said Mike's dad. "Mike and I can come back and give this whole section the attention it deserves when the museum is open."

"We can certainly give you the professional discount," offered Security Guard Broome, but it was obvious he wasn't happy about it.

As the conversation between the adults continued, Mike inspected the eggs. Was it his imagination, or were there little cracks on the shells?

Then, as if he were meant to see it, a tiny crack splintered down the egg closest to him. Mike jumped back.

"Is everything all right, son?" asked Mike's dad.

"Yes!" replied Mike.

Mike's dad turned to Dr. Giovanni. "Well, let's go see these fantastic underground facilities."

"Yes!" agreed Mike.

Mike quickly moved away from the display case. As he did, Security Guard Broome eyed him suspiciously.

They left the dinosaur gallery and headed toward a door marked Employees Only. Mike trailed behind his father and Dr. Giovanni. He reached into his Dino Jacket and pulled out his handheld video game system.

He quickly switched it on.

The message he received from Shannon after his last big adventure flashed up on the screen. But could he respond to it? Mike hoped his message would be received.

He typed,
"HELP! FOUND
T. REX EGGS!
THEY ARE ABOUT
TO HATCH!"

"Are you coming?" asked his father.

"What? Oh! Yes! Sorry." Mike smiled and held up his video game. "I was in the middle of a game."

Mike headed toward the stairs with his dad. He glanced back one last time at Security Guard Broome. Broome was glaring at him.

Mike really, really hoped his message got through to his friend Shannon.

Chapter 2

ALL CRACKED UP

The laboratory was freezing.

Mike was glad he was wearing his Dino Jacket. It was an awesome present from his dad. His dad and a friend designed the jacket to look exactly as though it was covered in dino scales.

The jacket also had tons of cool features that Mike was still discovering.

Mike clicked a button on the inside of the jacket, and three diamond shapes popped out of the back, like the plates on the back of a Stegosaurus. They were actually solar panels and helped heat the inside of his jacket.

"Sorry about the cool temperature in here," said Dr. Giovanni.

"Nothing to worry about, Doctor. Your facilities are truly state of the art," said Mike's dad, impressed.

Dr. Giovanni was just as excited to have Mike's dad there. "Your findings and research in the field are why we are able to do the work we do," he replied.

While the grown-ups talked, Mike couldn't help but worry. What could be happening upstairs in the dinosaur gallery? He needed a better look at those eggs. You would think that would be easy. After all, they were *his* eggs!

"Oh, Dr. Evans, let me show you our newest piece of equipment . . ." Dr. Giovanni said as he ushered them farther into the lab.

Mike knew this was his chance to slip away.

Under normal circumstances, Mike would never do anything like this. But these were not normal circumstances.

In fact, since his first dino dig, Mike's life had been anything but normal. Soon after, he had realized that the eggs might belong to the runaway T. rex he and Shannon had captured. Now there were four eggs in the museum about to hatch four baby Tyrannosaurus rex!

That was a problem.

A BIG problem!

Mike reached the top of the stairs and peered around the corner at the entrance of the dinosaur gallery. His main obstacle was Mr. Broome.

How am I going to get past him? Mike thought.

Mike looked around. *Perfect!*

The security guard desk. That would be his best chance. Sitting behind it was a guard much younger than Security Guard Broome. Not only that, but he seemed to be the opposite of Broome.

Broome was very serious about his job. This security guard did not seem so serious. He sat slumped in his chair with his feet up on the desk.

Mike knew that if he did that at home, his mother would immediately tell him to sit up straight.

INFORMATION

SECURI

The guard was playing with the volume button on his two-way radio while reading a comic book. Mike could use that radio to call Broome away from his post.

Mike stealthily made his way to the desk. He was close enough to grab the radio, but he still had to figure out how he was going to get it.

Mike was crouched down in front of the desk, unseen by the guard, who was more interested in his comic book than anything else. If anyone walked in, they would see Mike immediately.

He had to act fast!

Mike looked down at his jacket. This was a good time to try out another one of its features. He slowly moved his hands up to the hood's drawstrings.

Mike positioned himself directly in front of a stand fifteen feet away that held pamphlets, maps, and information about the museum. He pulled at the drawstrings, extending them out with his arms as far as they would go.

When Mike pulled the strings, two streams of water shot from the collar of the jacket like a powerful squirt gun.

SPLOOSH! Direct hit! The stand fell over with a tremendous crash.

The guard stood. Mike could see the name Nelson on the man's badge.

Mike moved around the security desk as Nelson came out from behind it to investigate. Mike grabbed the radio Nelson had left behind and then quickly made his escape.

Mike made his way back to the dinosaur gallery. Broome was still standing guard, but he was far enough down the hall that he couldn't see or hear Mike.

Mike turned on the radio and whispered, "Hello."

He heard his voice crackle from Security Guard Broome's radio. Broome pulled his radio from his belt. "Come again, over," he said.

Mike had lowered the volume on his radio so that no one else could hear Broome's voice come through.

He waited.

Broome spoke again. "Nelson? Is that you? How many times have I told you that this radio is not a toy!"

Mike pressed the button and mumbled into the radio.

"Nelson, you haven't handcuffed yourself to your chair again, have you?" he said, waiting for a response.

Mike didn't answer.

Broome barked into his radio as he finally walked away from his post. "How many times have I told you that our security equipment is not a toy! This is the last time I'm going to uncuff you, and this time we're filling out a report."

Mike did not want to see Nelson get in trouble for something he didn't do, but this was important. He ran into the dinosaur gallery and immediately went to the egg display.

He was too late.

The dinosaurs had already hatched!

Chapter 3

RADIO BUTTERFLIES

Four baby T. rex were running around inside the display case. Each one was about the size of a small chicken.

Any minute the security guards would figure out something wasn't right. They would barge in and find him with four **BABY DINOSAURS!**

What was Mike going to do?

"Think!" Mike told himself.

Mike reached into his Dino Jacket. He pulled out . . . his underwear!

When he was packing for his trip to New York City, his mother made such a big deal about bringing extra clean underwear and socks. He even stuffed extras into the large, hidden pockets of his jacket.

Mike quickly emptied his pockets of all his underwear and then lifted the cover to the display case.

He carefully wrangled each of the baby dinos and placed them, one at a time, into his jacket pockets.

Once they were secured inside his pockets, the dinos began to wiggle, claw, and chomp. He was glad the jacket was made of bite-proof material!

Then Mike quickly smooshed his extra underwear and socks into the broken egg shells, making them look as if they were still whole.

Mike replaced the display glass. If no one came within five feet of them, they wouldn't be able to tell the difference. No one would be the wiser!

"Where do you think you're going?" came the booming voice of Security Guard Broome.

Mike froze in his tracks. He looked down at his overstuffed, wriggling jacket. Then he noticed he was still holding Nelson's radio. He quickly tried to hide it behind his back, but Mike knew Broome must have seen it.

"You are not supposed to be here! And I'm fairly certain you're the culprit behind Nelson's missing radio."

"I can explain —" began Mike.

Broome wasn't listening. He was scanning the gallery for anything out of the ordinary. His eyes locked on the egg display case.

Then the guard looked down at Mike's Dino Jacket. Not only was it bigger than last time, but now it was also moving! Broome reached down and grabbed the zipper of Mike's jacket. Mike shut his eyes in anticipation.

Broome opened the jacket.

Four baby T. rex leaped from the open jacket and landed on Broome!

Baby T. rex don't weigh much, but the surprise knocked Broome over.

"Ah!" he screamed as he went down. The four baby dinosaurs scattered in different directions. "D-D-Dinosaurs?!"

"No . . ." Mike tried to explain, "they're lizards . . ." In a lower voice he added, "That will grow to tremendous size and be able to eat you in one gulp."

"I was told to expect a possible dinosaur," said Broome, "but *four* baby T. rex?!"

Mike knew it! Broome must have been sent by his enemy Jurassic Jeff! How else could he have known to expect a real dinosaur?

Mike definitely had to get the baby dinosaurs back now. He ran after them.

"Get back here!" said Broome as he lunged after Mike.

"Nelson!" Broome yelled over the radio. "He's heading down the hall and into the Butterfly Conservatory."

Sure enough, Mike turned the corner and followed the baby T. rex into the Butterfly Conservatory. The T. rex ran through the automatic doors into a hot, sticky, humid room full of plants, trees, and butterflies.

Immediately, each baby T. rex began snapping at every colorful butterfly that crossed it.

Chomp! Chomp! Chomp!

Once inside, Mike folded down one of the tropical tree branches. He wrapped it around the handles of the automatic doors.

Broome ran in from the other side and smacked right into the doors, expecting them to open automatically.

Getting back up, he tried to manually force the doors open, but Mike had done a good job securing them.

Mike turned to grab the T. rex. They were still busy snapping unsuccessfully at passing butterflies. He was surprised to see Security Guard Nelson nearby!

"Whoa!" said Nelson. "That little dude looks just like a real dinosaur!"

Security Guard Nelson dove for the baby T. rex just as Mike noticed a gift shop full of butterfly nets. According to the museum guide pamphlet, visitors were allowed to capture butterflies with the nets to study them and then release them unharmed.

Mike grabbed one of the nets. Instead of catching butterflies, he used it to catch Nelson! The net went over Nelson's head and obscured his vision. Then Mike grabbed a second net and used it to capture the T. rex.

Having one in the net, Mike looked
around for the other baby dinosaurs.
They were running out the opposite end
of the Butterfly Conservatory. Mike went
after them before Nelson and Broome
could get organized enough to follow.

Mike exited the butterfly enclosure and headed back down the hall toward the dinosaur wing. He knew he was on the fourth floor. He had to round up the dinosaurs, get down to the first floor, and leave the museum without any security guards, any research scientists, or his dad finding out.

That would be the easy part. But what was he going to do with T. rex babies even if got out?

"Stop!" came a voice from behind.

Mike froze in his tracks. *So much for not getting caught,* he thought.

Chapter 4

JUPITER SMUPITER

Mike stood as still a statue. The only movement was the squirming of the T. rex in the butterfly net. If only Shannon had gotten his message . . .

"Mike, is that you? It's me. Shannon!"

Mike was shocked. He turned to see his friend. The person he thought, for a split second, that he had imagined.

Shannon was dressed much differently than when he had last seen her. Back then, she dressed to blend into the forest. Today, she had on a shimmery gold top and designer jeans.

"You got my message!" said Mike happily as he greeted her.

Shannon looked confused. "What message?"

Before Mike could answer, Security Guard Nelson appeared behind them.

"Run!" said Mike as he grabbed Shannon by the hand and sprinted down the hall. Nelson followed, still trying to get the butterfly net off his face.

As they moved down the hall, away from the dinosaur gallery, Mike saw a sign labeled Audubon Gallery.

"Let's see if we can lose him in the bird section," he said.

"What's going on?" asked Shannon.

Before Mike could answer, Shannon saw a small baby T. rex standing near the stairwell. She stopped and pointed. "What is that?" she asked.

"Another T. rex!" Mike replied.

Mike quickly scooped up the baby T. rex into the butterfly net with the other one. The two barely fit. He would need something else to put them in.

"Another T. rex?" asked Shannon. "How many are there?"

"You remember our little adventure with the dinosaur we named Sam?" Mike said distractedly as he secured the dinosaur and headed down the stairs toward the third floor.

"How can I forget?" said Shannon.

"Well, after you left, I found four eggs very close to the dig site —"

"OH MY GOSH!" Shannon shouted. "Samantha! That T. rex was a girl!"

They both jumped off the last remaining steps and landed near a sign that read Planetarium.

Signs all over the door to the planetarium said the exhibit was closed for reconstruction. They ducked inside anyway and shut the door behind them.

"Whew!" Mike exclaimed. He slid down to the floor, slumping against the wall. He pointed to the squirming butterfly net beside him.

"There were four eggs altogether," explained Mike. "They hatched just a little while ago. I captured these two, but there are two more on the loose."

SCREEEEEEEEEEEEEECH!

Just then, a high-pitched squeal came from above their heads.

Mike and Shannon both looked up. Above them twirled models of the planets in the solar system. Atop the planet Jupiter stood another baby T. rex.

"I think we just found another one," said Shannon. "I'll climb up and get it."

"Wait," said Mike, grasping his hood's drawstrings. "I have a better idea."

For the second time that day, Mike tugged on his drawstrings, releasing a burst of water. The stream struck the T. rex, blasting it off the planet above.

Thinking quickly, Shannon readied herself beneath the falling dino like a baseball outfielder. She grabbed the tiny beast out of midair with ease.

"Nice catch!" Mike exclaimed.

"Yeah, but now what?" she asked.

Mike looked around. The room was under construction, and he spotted parts of planets scattered on the ground. Some were split into two equal parts, like two halves of a plastic Easter egg.

Mike grabbed two halves of the planet Saturn. He stuck one baby dino inside and then clicked the two halves together. A perfect fit! Mike did the same for the other two dinosaurs they had already captured.

"That should hold them until we track down the last one," Mike said.

Mike and Shannon started walking toward the planetarium exit. "I'm so glad you got my message," added Mike.

"Message? I still don't know what you're talking about," replied Shannon, "I'm here to —"

Just as they reached the exit, the doors suddenly burst open. They both jumped back in surprise.

"I've got you now!" said Security Guard Broome.

Chapter 5

DINO FAMILY

"UNCLE RENO!" exclaimed
Shannon, leaping into Broome's arm.

"Triceratops?" replied the security
guard, surprised to see her.

Triceratops was Shannon's nickname.
Only her family called her that. They
were related?

"You're early!" Broome said.

Shannon finally let him go and said, "I thought I would surprise you!"

"You know each other?" Mike asked.

Broome turned to Mike. "You little hooligan!" he said, pointing an accusing finger. "You've got a lot to answer for!"

"Wait, Uncle Reno," said Shannon. "This is my friend Mike."

Broome stopped. "Your friend?"

"Yes," Shannon answered. "This is the friend who helped me capture that T. rex a few weeks ago."

56

"I thought he might be with Jeff," said Broome.

"Jurassic Jeff?" replied Mike in his own defense. "No way!"

"Then why have you been running all over the museum, stealing radios and causing trouble?" demanded Broome.

"When my dad found out about the eggs, he wanted to bring them here. I had no idea they were going to hatch!" Mike thought for a second and then turned to Shannon. "If you didn't know I was in trouble, then why are you here?"

"My uncle contacted me when the eggs were delivered here," she said.

Broome added, "I heard about the trouble you had with Jeff, so I thought there might be something more to all this . . . and apparently, I was right."

"Well, it's lucky that we're all here to take care of this problem," said Shannon. "Of the four dinos that hatched, Mike has capture three." She pointed to the wiggling planets nearby.

Broome looked at his watch. "We have half an hour before the museum opens," he said.

Broome opened the door to exit the planetarium and came face to face with Security Guard Nelson.

Remnants of the broken butterfly net were still tangled on his head.

"Hey!" exclaimed Nelson. "I found you! For a second I thought maybe the butterflies had done you in!" Then Nelson pointed to Mike and said, "Isn't that the kid we're looking for, Broome?"

"Yes it is," replied Broome. "Good job, Nelson. Now back to your post."

As they all filed past Nelson, Mike handed him back his radio. "I think this belongs to you," he said.

Nelson smiled. "Thanks, little dude. I've been looking for this." Then he said, "Hey, by the way, what happened to those little iguanas you were chasing?"

Chapter 6

GONE FISHING

They searched almost everywhere.

"This is the last gallery," said Mike as he pulled open the heavy doors that led to the Oceans of Life gallery.

"What happens if the dino's not in here?" asked Shannon.

"I guess we'll have to deal with that when we get to it, but hopefully —"

Mike didn't even have to finish his sentence. The baby T. rex was running back and forth in front of the large aquarium, chasing the fish.

Shannon raised her finger to her lips. The T. rex hadn't spotted them yet. If they kept quiet, they could probably sneak up on it.

SCREEEEEEEEEEEEEEECH!

Suddenly, the T. rex spotted Shannon's glittery shirt. It lunged forward, snapping its pointy teeth.

Shannon slowly took a step back. But the T. rex took off, running full speed at her.

Shannon sprinted away like a football player. She zigged and zagged, leaping over benches and displays, but the T. rex was hot on her trail.

Mike looked up. Among the ocean life displays on the walls and ceiling, he spotted a large fishing net. "I have an idea," he yelled toward Shannon.

Mike scrambled up a nearby flight of stairs to a second-floor walkway. He tried reaching for the netting, which was draped across the ceiling above him. It was just out of his grasp.

"Any help would be appreciated!" Shannon yelled out as she kept running.

"Hang on!" Mike said.

Without a second thought, Mike stepped onto the walkway's guardrail. He balanced on the edge, twenty feet above the floor below. A split second later, Mike leaped from the banister and grabbed hold of the netting.

Mike watched Shannon zigzag below him, the baby T. rex still hot on her trail. At just the right moment, he released a set of razor-sharp claws from the cuffs of his jacket. The claws tore through the net, sending Mike toward the floor.

"Look out below!" Mike yelled as he fell with the net.

Ker-pluff!! Mike landed in the gift shop display of dolphin plush toys. The net landed on top of Shannon and the T. rex, trapping them inside.

"Eek!" Shannon screamed.

Mike scrambled out of the toy bin. He helped Shannon out from under the net but kept the dino trapped inside.

"We got it!" Mike exclaimed.

"Yeah, we did," replied Shannon. "But the museum is now open. How are we going to get it out of here?"

"I have another idea!" replied Mike.

"Oh great . . ." Shannon sighed.

Chapter 7

BLAST FROM THE PAST

Mike and Shannon stepped out of the Oceans of Life gallery. Dozens of museum goers funneled into the main entrance. Security Guard Broome ushered them inside.

"I assume everything is under control?" he asked Mike and Shannon.

"Mostly," Shannon replied.

"Where is the . . ." Security Guard
Broome lowered his voice, "T. rex."

Mike held a large plush dolphin. The
toy suddenly jerked in his arms and let
out a high-pitched **SQUEEEEEEAK!**

"He's in there?" asked
Broome.

Mike smiled. "We had
to get, um, creative," he
explained.

"We'll wait upstairs until museum hours are over," added Shannon. "Then we take all of the dinos to the *Atlantica*."

"That would be best," Broome said. "I'll meet you upstairs as soon as I can."

Mike and Shannon moved through the crowd with the undercover dino.

"What's the *Atlantica*?" Mike asked.

"I probably shouldn't have mentioned that," Shannon replied.

"After everything we've been through, you still won't tell me about your secret dinosaur society?" asked Mike, upset.

"I didn't want the information falling into the wrong hands," Shannon said.

Mike said, "You mean —?"

"Jeff," interrupted Shannon.

"Yeah, that's what I was going say," replied Mike.

"No," said Shannon, pointing at the other side of the museum. "It's Jeff!"

Sitting on a bench holding a museum map was the boy who started this whole mess by setting a live T. rex loose on their last adventure. He was the one responsible for four baby dinos now running free . . .

JURASSIC JEFF!

Jeff spotted Mike and Shannon. He gave them an evil glare.

Suddenly, the plush dolphin jerked and slipped from Mike's hands. It flopped and hopped on the floor like a fish out of water. Mike scooped up the toy before anyone could notice — except one person.

Jeff was still staring at them. He gave Mike and Shannon a knowing wink.

"He knows," Mike whispered to Shannon. "We need to get all the dinos out of the museum . . . NOW!"

"How?" asked Shannon. "The entire museum is filled with visitors."

Mike grabbed Shannon's arm. "We'll figure out something," he told her.

The duo made a mad dash for the planetarium. They weaved through the crowd. Jeff was right on their tail.

Mike and Shannon rushed inside the planetarium. **Wham!** They slammed the door behind them and braced against it.

"What are we going to do?" asked Shannon.

"I don't know," replied Mike. "It's like he's been watching us the whole time!"

Just then, Shannon and Mike noticed a man in the middle of the planetarium. He was standing near the model planets that had the other dinosaurs hidden inside.

Nelson smiled. "Hey, little dude and dudette," he said, "I found your precious little iguanas."

Chapter 8

SAY IT, DON'T SPRAY IT

"Two against two," said Jeff as he came into the planetarium behind them. He stepped toward Mike and Shannon.

"I'm not a cruel person," he said. "I don't want to release these dinos inside the museum. I'd rather do it out there in Central Park. Or better yet, in Montana, where I wanted them in first place."

"But why?" Mike asked.

"I'm giving them a second chance at life," said Jeff. "A chance to thrive."

"But think about how much damage this is going to do to our planet," Shannon pleaded. "Don't do it, Jeff."

"You're just scared because you can't stop me!" said Jeff with a smirk.

Mike held up his arms in surrender. "You're right," he told Jeff. "I don't think we can win."

"Ha!" Jeff laughed. "Look, Shannon, even your buddy is giving up!"

Shannon, surprised, stared at Mike. "What are you doing?" she asked.

Then Shannon noticed that Mike was
holding the drawstrings of his hoodie.

"THIS!" Mike exclaimed.

Mike pulled the strings again,
unleashing his secret weapon. Streams
of water shot from his Dino Jacket.

SPA-LOOSH!

The streams blasted Nelson in the face. Mike took the opportunity to grab one of the dino-filled planets away from him. At the same time, Shannon snagged Nelson's walkie-talkie.

Once Jeff realized what Mike was doing, he rolled the Saturn model away from them and toward the exit. Mike and Shannon followed after him.

Shannon pushed a button on the radio. "Uncle Reno!"

"Shannon?" answered his voice. "What are you doing on the radio?"

"Nelson has been working for Jeff!" she told him.

"JEFF?" came the confused response. "How do you know?"

"Because Jeff is here, and he is currently rolling Saturn outside to Central Park," answered Shannon. "I'm right behind him, and we just left the planetarium!"

"I'll be right there!" said Broome.

Jeff and Mike were rolling the model planets down the hallway. There were more people than before. They stopped and stared at the two young boys rolling planets past them. Although they stopped to look, not many people seemed too bothered by event.

Jeff steered his planet to the top of the stairs. With a push, he tipped it over the edge and watched as it bounced down the stairs. Mike was headed in the same direction, but then he spotted something. Right down the hall, about twenty feet away from the stairs, the doors to the elevator opened.

"This way!" said Mike as he rolled the planet right into the elevator. Seeing Jupiter hurtling toward them, the museum goers inside the elevator moved to one side or the other. The planet stopped when it bumped the back of the elevator. Mike came to a skidding stop, turned to the person closest to the buttons, and said, "First floor, please."

"We're heading to the first floor!" exclaimed Shannon as she ran full speed at the elevator.

She barely squeezed through the closing doors. Mike caught her as she fell into his arms.

"Hey," she said, realizing there were other people in the elevator with them.

"What's up?" replied Mike.

They both tried to remain calm and not let anyone know that there were dinosaurs inside the Jupiter model.

"Jeff took the stairs," said Mike. "I thought this might be faster."

The old lady with the umbrella next to Mike gave him a look.

Mike smiled at her and said, "They're a matching set. The other planet should be downstairs when we get there."

The elevator doors opened. As they did, Broome came running up to it.

"Where is he?" asked Broome.

Just then, the planet Saturn came bouncing down the stairs followed directly by Jeff.

"We're going after him!" said Shannon. "The planet and the dolphin in here have the you-know-what inside."

Broome turned to everyone in the elevator and said, "Sorry, folks, this elevator is no longer in service!"

As people filed out, Broome took out his keys and locked the elevator door shut with the dinosaurs inside. Mike and Shannon had positioned themselves between Jeff and the exit.

Jeff brought the planet to a rolling stop. He shifted his eyes back and forth, scouting the room.

"It's over Jeff. There's nowhere to go," said Mike.

"The boy's right," said Broome, moving behind Jeff.

"I don't know about that," said Jeff. "I might have an option or two left."

Mike thought Jeff had no option but to give up. He was wrong.

Jeff reached out to the display next to the bottom of the stairwell. The prehistoric man in the display was holding a crude type of hammer made from a rock strapped to a stick. Jurassic Jeff grabbed the hammer and held it high above his head.

"So much for no options," said Mike.

Before any of them could react, Jeff brought the hammer down on the model planet. It broke open into two pieces.

Chapter 9
DINO SCRAMBLE

There was stunned silence on the first floor of the museum. For a few seconds, no one made a sound. Everyone was staring at just one thing.

The baby T. rex had been released from its hiding place. Jurassic Jeff had just unleashed a live dinosaur in the middle of New York City!

The silence was finally broken when the dinosaur opened its mouth and let out a screech. **REEEEEEEEEE!!**

People in the museum started to run in every direction, shrieking and waving their hands in the air.

Jeff herded the T. rex toward the front door. The tiny T. rex talons clacked on the marble tiled floor.

Mike and Shannon followed behind him. Security Guard Broome went into crowd control mode, so people would not hurt each other.

"I can't believe he did that!" said Shannon.

"From what I know about this guy, I don't think there is anything he wouldn't do!" replied Mike.

By the time they got outside, Mike and Shannon could see Jeff guiding the T. rex across the street. He was even using the crosswalk.

Taxis were honking, and people were moving away from the T. rex. Looking to the other side of the street, Mike saw the trees and greenery of Central Park. The giant park was surrounded by concrete in the middle of the city.

"If he gets to the park, we may never find that T. rex again," said Shannon.

Then, an idea from a past adventure hit Mike. "I've got it!" he exclaimed.

On the other side of the street, right before the entrance to the park, there was a hot dog cart. There were also a bunch of other booths set up on either side of it selling a range of items like artwork, cheap jewelry, and even hats and T-shirts for tourists.

"How much money do you have on you?" asked Mike.

"What? What for?" asked Shannon.

Mike stopped and took all his money out of his pockets and shoved it at the hot dog vendor.

"Oh!" said Shannon, realizing why he needed the money. "You're thinking what mama T. rex likes, baby T. rex likes!"

"Exactly!" exclaimed Mike.

"Would you like mustard or ketchup?" asked the hot dog vendor.

"Neither! And you can forget the buns too! I just need the hot dogs — uncooked please!" said Mike.

The hotdog vendor looked at Mike and then shrugged, "I've had stranger requests, kids." He piled twenty hot dogs into a small cardboard box and handed them to the duo.

Inside the park gates, Mike and Shannon looked for Jeff and the T. rex. They were just outside the tree line.

"He's almost free!" shouted Jeff, laughing at them. "Once he's loose in the park, you'll never find him!"

SPLAT!

"What the —"
was the only thing a
stunned Jeff could say.

After another
second he said, "Did you just hit me in
the head with a hot dog?"

"Yeah, sorry about that," said Mike
as he continued to lob hot dogs over
Jeff's head. "I was actually trying to get
that one over you."

Jeff was confused. "Why?"

"Roar!" came a sound from behind.

Jeff turned to see that the tiny T. rex
was snapping up the hot dogs as fast as
Mike could throw them.

Jeff said, "Very funny. But as soon as you run out of hot dogs, he'll leave."

Shannon looked at the box of hot dogs Mike was holding. It was true. Mike was down to half of what he started with. Shannon looked down at her shirt and then back at the T-shirt vendors right outside the park gates.

"Fine. I'll wait!" said Jeff. "Finish your little feeding and then watch as this little guy goes out into the world and grows to full size in the middle of New York City!" Jeff laughed.

"Oh, I don't know about that!" said Shannon, running toward Jeff.

Mike saw her run by and realized she was dressed a little differently. She was now wearing an I Love NY T-shirt, with a big red heart on it.

Above her head, she was waving her sparkling, shimmery shirt. She looped the gold shirt over Jeff's head.

"What's this?" asked Jeff, inspecting the shirt that was now around his neck. "This isn't exactly my color."

"It's not for you," replied Shannon. "It's for him."

They all turned to look at the T. rex. Mike noticed the T. rex was staring at the sparkly shirt.

He had seen the same crazy look in its eye when it had chased Shannon around the aquarium.

It thought there was a fish around Jeff's neck.

The T. rex leaped at Jeff. It knocked him over and pinned him to the ground.

It stood on Jeff's chest and pulled at the shirt around his neck with its jaws.

"Ahhhhh! Get it off me! It's going to eat me!" yelled Jeff.

"Only if you promise to stop this crazy plan of yours to repopulate the Earth with dinosaurs!" said Shannon.

Jeff, tired of having his head and chest slammed on the ground, agreed quickly. "Okay! I promise. I will do whatever you want!"

Mike was skeptical. "How do you know he's telling the truth?"

"I don't know," admitted Shannon, "but I don't want him to get eaten."

"Good point," said Mike. "How do we get it off him?"

Shannon smiled and handed Mike a couple of New York City tourist shirts. "I forgot to tell you . . . I always keep some emergency money in my shoe."

"Nice," said Mike.

"Besides," she said, "you should never come to New York City without buying a few souvenirs."

Chapter 10
MOVIE HERO

Shannon purchased three more I Love NY shirts. Two were being used as a netting to completely cover and contain the baby dino. The last one Shannon had used to tie Jeff's hands behind his back, so he wouldn't try to steal the dinosaur again.

They headed back to the museum.

Mike expected to see the place cleared out or the police or maybe even his father. What Mike did not expect was the round of applause that greeted them as they walked in. All the people that were running around scared when the T. rex broke loose from the model were now cheering and clapping.

Security Guard Broome came running up to them when he saw them.

"Ha! There you are!" said Broome, talking to the crowd as he gestured to the three of them. "Don't you think they did a splendid job? They had some of you scared, I bet!"

The applause got even louder.

Broome continued, "Thank you, ladies and gentlemen, thank you! Remember to catch the movie in theatres this summer — Dinosaur Park is going to be a huge box-office hit!"

Shannon guided Jeff through the lobby, and Mike struggled against a fidgeting pile of I Love NY T-shirts. When they were well out of earshot from anyone else, Shannon said, "What was all that about, Uncle Reno?"

"Everyone was so panicked when that little T. rex burst out of that ball, so I told them it was just a movie stunt."

"What?" asked Mike and Jeff at the same time.

"I told them it was a publicity stunt. You know, like something a studio would do to attract attention for their movie. They all immediately calmed down."

"So now they don't even believe it's a real dinosaur?" asked Jeff, still not willing to accept what he had just heard from Broome.

"You should be ashamed of yourself! What you did here was a horrible thing! Do you know how many people could have been hurt?" said Broome.

"It was worth it! Dinosaurs need to roam free just like people do. Don't worry though, I'll make it happen . . . someday!" Jeff promised.

"No, you won't!" snapped Shannon. "You've done nothing but cause trouble for weeks now."

"I'm sure you are going to be in a world of trouble once Henry finds out what you've been doing," Security Guard Broome chimed in.

"Henry? Who's Henry?" asked Mike.

Shannon tried to get Broome's attention before it was too late.

"Henry? He's my brother and Shannon and Jeff's father."

It was too late. He had just said what Shannon was trying so desperately to keep from Mike.

"WHAT?" said Mike, this time as an actual question and with a lot more surprise. He turned to Shannon. "Wait, your father? Jeff is your brother?"

Shannon smiled and turned a bright red that almost matched her hair.

Jeff also smiled since the first time they had captured him in the park. "You never told him we're related?" he said.

Shannon was looking at the ground as they walked up the stairs to the planetarium. "No . . . but it's not because I didn't want to," she said.

"I'm sorry, honey. I didn't know," apologized Security Guard Broome.

"No, it's okay. If anyone deserves to know, it's Mike. He's been so helpful both here and in Montana. Without him, Jeff would have reintroduced dinosaurs back into the world."

"Thanks . . . I think," said Mike. "I guess after everything we've been through, I would have thought it might be worth mentioning that Jurassic Jeff was your brother."

By this time, they had arrived at the planetarium entrance.

Jeff decided to speak up. "You think you stopped me, but you haven't!" he yelled. "I've got friends everywhere!"

"If you're talking about your friend Nelson, I fired him. He was escorted by my security from the premises while you were making trouble in the park," Security Guard Broome reported.

This bit of news seemed to shut down any other outbursts from Jeff.

"Yes, I thought that might quiet you down for a while," said Broome as he escorted Jeff into the planetarium.

Mike and Shannon remained outside.

"Mike, I wanted —" Shannon began, but Mike cut her off as he handed her the baby dinosaur wrapped in T-shirts.

"It's okay. I understand," said Mike.

Mike put on his best fake smile. "You couldn't even tell me that the bad guy we were chasing was your brother."

"He's been horrible since we —" she stopped herself before she could finish the sentence.

Mike decided to understand as much as she would let him. "I get it. Dinosaur secrets. Your dad is probably the president of the United States or something." Before Shannon could answer, Mike spoke up again. "Your scary uncle is probably the only one in your family with a normal job . . . unless he's a super-secret spy or something."

Shannon laughed. "No, he's a real security guard here at the museum. He has been for almost forty years. It's kind of how my dad became interested in dinosaurs."

She stopped smiling.

There was a long and awkward pause.

"So, I guess you and your dad will be taking care of the baby T. rex," Mike finally said.

"Yeah, we'll make sure they get back to Sam."

"You mean *Samantha*," Mike reminded her.

There was another long pause.

"Well," said Mike. "Speaking of dads, I better go find mine. He's probably wondering what kind of trouble I've been getting into. But don't worry! I won't tell him anything."

Mike zipped up his Dino Jacket and turned to leave. "See you around," he said to her. Then he turned the corner and headed down the stairs.

He didn't hear Shannon as she waved and said, "Bye."

***

"Hey, Dad," said Mike as he walked
into the research facilities in the
basement of the museum. Mike's dad
and Dr. Giovanni were looking into a
large microscope. They had papers and
microscope slides spread out.

"Hey, buddy. Where've you been?"

"Oh, just out and around," replied Mike.

"In the museum? I hope Security Guard Broome didn't hassle you too much," said Dr. Giovanni.

"No," Mike replied, smiling. "As a matter of fact, he's not such a bad guy after all."

"Really?" said a surprised Dr. Giovanni. "He usually doesn't take a liking to many people."

"I bet that jacket didn't hurt in helping you make conversation," said his dad, pointing to the Dino Jacket.

"Yes, sir." Mike tugged on the jacket and said, "Trust me dad, this thing came in handy."

"It certainly did," said a deep voice from behind them.

Mike turned to find Security Guard Broom standing at the entrance to the research facility.

"I hope you will forgive the intrusion, Dr. Giovanni," Broome said. "But I have a guest who would like to meet Dr. Evans, if possible."

Shannon stepped out from behind Security Guard Broome. Mike was shocked to see her.

"Dr. Giovanni, I'd like to introduce you to my niece. This is Shannon Broome," continued Security Guard Broome.

"Pleased to meet you," said Dr. Giovanni, shaking her hand. "This is Dr. Stanley Evans and his son, Mike."

"Hello, Dr. Evans," said Shannon as she shook his hand. "I've heard so much about you."

"You have?" said Mike's dad as he gave Mike a surprised look.

"Yes. I've heard my father talk about you and your research often," replied Shannon.

"Your father?" asked Mike.

Shannon turned to Mike and said, "Yes, perhaps you've heard of him? Dr. Henry Broome?"

There was a definite change in the mood of the room. It was very still until Dr. Giovanni said, "Reno? Your brother is Henry Broome? Why have you never mentioned this before?"

"Ah, well, you see my brother is . . ."

"Dad is a very private person. A recluse, if you will," Shannon broke in.

"A what?" The question came from Mike before he realized he even asked it.

"Mike," said his father with a tone that indicated he should not have asked that question.

"No, it's okay. My father doesn't like the spotlight or public places very much. He likes to spend most of his time away from people."

"Dr. Broome is one of the world's foremost authorities on dinosaurs. His research is a must-read for anyone going into the paleontology field," added his dad.

"Correct," said Shannon. "And when he learned from Uncle Reno that you were coming here to New York City, Dr. Evans, he sent me with an invitation. My father would like to know if you would come meet with him." She then turned to Mike and continued, "Of course we would also extend the invitation to your son. My father has heard about his recent discovery of T. rex eggs."

"Um . . ." said Mike's father, which let everyone in the room know he was stunned by the invitation.

"I . . . we would like that very much," he finally managed to get out. "I heard rumors that he's living in Europe somewhere."

"Close," replied Shannon, "but more like *Atlantis*."

"Excuse me?" asked Mike's dad.

"He lives underwater." Shannon smiled and winked at Mike. "On a submarine in the Atlantic ocean."

Time for another adventure! thought Dino-Mike.

GLOSSARY

Jurassic Period (juh-RA-sik PlHR-ee-uhd)—a period of time about 200 to 144 million years ago

paleontologist (pale-ee-uhn-TOL-uh-gist)—a scientist who deals with fossils and other life-forms

planetarium (plan-uh-TAIR-ee-uhm)—a building with equipment for reproducing the positions and movements of the sun, moon, planets, and stars by projecting their images onto a curved ceiling

prehistoric (pree-hi-STOR-ik)—belonging to a time before history was recorded

triceratops (try-SER-uh-tops)—a large, plant-eating dinosaur with three horns and a fan-shaped collar of bone

tyrannosaurus (ti-RAN-uh-sor-uhs)—a large, meat-eating dinosaur that walked on its hind legs, also known as a T. rex

DINO FACTS!

Did you know you can tell a plant-eating dinosaur from a meat-eater by noting how many legs they walked on? Plant-eaters typically stomped around on all four legs. Swift and deadly meat-eaters often hunted on two.

Tyrannosaurus rex had a mouthful of deadly teeth, which were shaped like bananas. But what's with those puny arms? Dino experts think the tiny paws meant that T. rex didn't fight for its food but ate creatures that were already dead. Yuck!

At least one T. rex has left its poop behind. Scientist examined the fossilized feces and found bone fragments from a Triceratops.

The first fossilized dinosaur eggs ever found were discovered in France in 1869. Even today, these eggs remain the largest ever found, weighing up to fifteen pounds and measuring more than a foot long.

What does the word "dinosaur" mean? The word comes from the Greek language and means "terrible lizard." In 1842, paleontologist Richard Owen was the first person to call dinosaurs by this name.

The world's tallest dinosaur fossil is displayed at Museum für Naturkunde, Berlin's natural history museum. The Brachiosaurus stands forty-one feet, five inches high.

ABOUT THE AUTHOR

Bronx, New York–born writer and artist Franco Aureliani has been drawing comics since he could hold a crayon. Currently residing in upstate New York with his wife, Ivette, and son, Nicolas, he spends most of his days in his Batcave-like studio where he works on comics projects. In 1995, Franco founded Blindwolf Studios, an independent art studio where he and fellow creators can create children's comics. Franco is the creator, artist, and writer of Weirdsville, L'il Creeps, and Eagle All Star, as well as the cocreator and writer of Patrick the Wolf Boy.

Franco recently finished work on Superman Family Adventures, and is now cowriting the series The Green Team: Teen Trillionaires and Tiny Titans by DC Comics. When he's not writing and drawing, Franco teaches high school art.